Armin Greder

THE ISLAND

ALLEN&UNWIN

One morning, the people of the island found a man on the beach,
where fate and ocean currents had washed his raft ashore.
When he saw them coming, he stood up.

He wasn't like them.

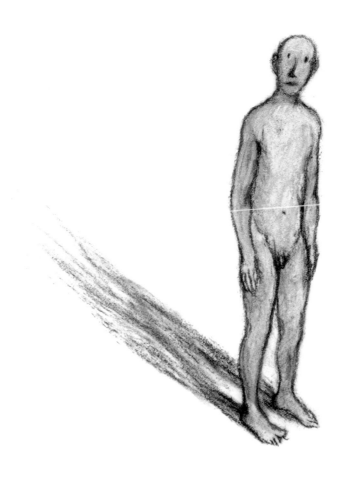

The people stared at him. They were puzzled.
Why had he come here? What did he want? What should they do?
One of them suggested it would be best to put the man straight back
on his raft and send him away without delay.
'I am sure he wouldn't like it here, so far away from his own kind.'

But the fisherman knew the sea.
'If we send him back, it will be
the death of him and I don't want
that on my conscience,' he said.
'We have to take him in.'

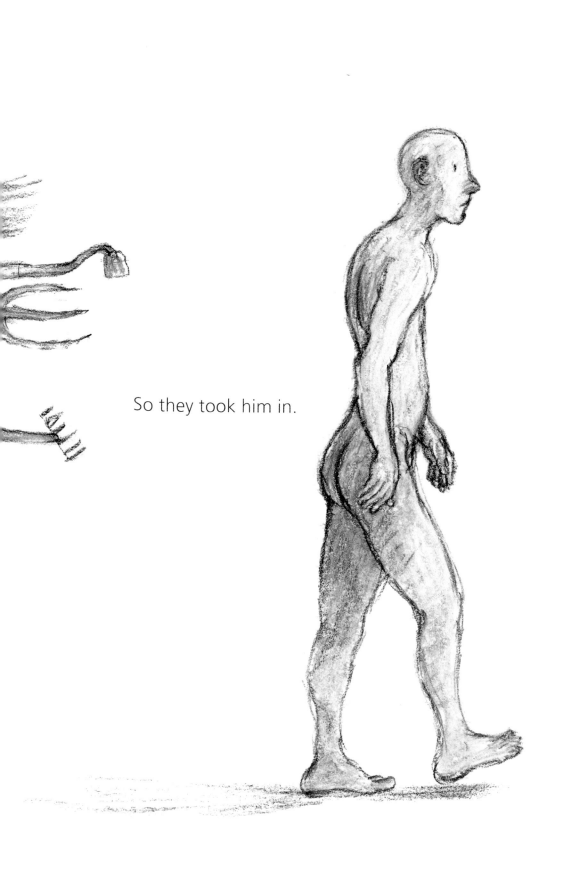

So they took him in.

They took him to the uninhabited part of the island, to a goat pen that had been empty for a long time. They made him understand that he was to stay there and showed him where he could sleep on some straw.

And then they locked the gate and went back to their business, and life on the island returned to what it had always been.

Then one morning the man appeared in town.

This caused a commotion.

The people grabbed him roughly and screamed at him. He tried to make them understand that he was hungry, that he hadn't eaten for days, and could they not give him something to eat.

'He is right,' said the fisherman. 'We can't ignore him now that he is among us. We must help him.'

This frightened the people.

'But we can't just feed anyone who comes our way,' argued the grocer. 'We don't have enough for everyone. We would all starve to death!'

The fisherman suggested that someone should give him a job so that he could earn his keep. 'And,' he added quietly, 'he would probably work for less pay than one of us.'

The innkeeper could surely use some help in the kitchen?

'If he was in my kitchen, nobody would want to eat at my inn,' muttered the innkeeper. 'Hire him yourself!'

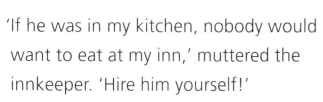

But there was only room for one on the fisherman's boat.

The carpenter remembered the man's poorly crafted raft. He evidently had no idea how to use a hammer or saw.

e carter said simply, 'Look at him! I need
neone who can carry heavy loads.'

And the priest was very sorry, but the
stranger's voice would clash with the rest
of the choir.

that case we will have to look after him together,' said the fisherman.
e took him in. We can't turn our backs. Even though he is not one of us,
is still our responsibility.'

In the end, the innkeeper agreed to let the man have the scraps he would otherwise toss to the pigs, and they took him back to the goat pen. They strengthened the gate and took turns to guard him, so that in future he would not disturb them.

But despite this the man's presence continued to trouble the people.

They hadn't asked for him, but he was here. Their act of kindness had not been the end, merely a beginning. They had taken him onto their island and now he was part of their lives.

He haunted their days and often their dreams. Men frowned and muttered under their breaths. Women stayed in their kitchens, and mothers warned their children not to go near the goat pen.

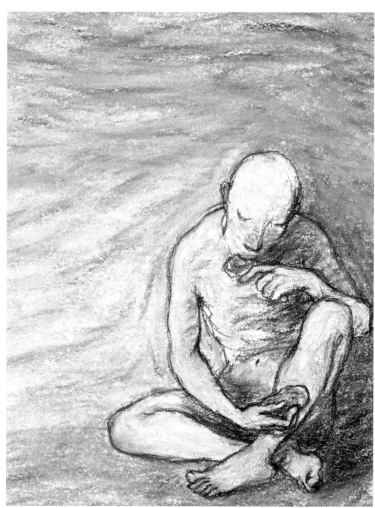

e school teacher lectured about savages
d their strange ways.

'He eats with his hands,' said the innkeeper.
'And he eats bones!'

'He will come and eat you if you don't finish your soup!' a mother warned her child.

'The children are scared of him,' lamented the school teacher that night at the inn.

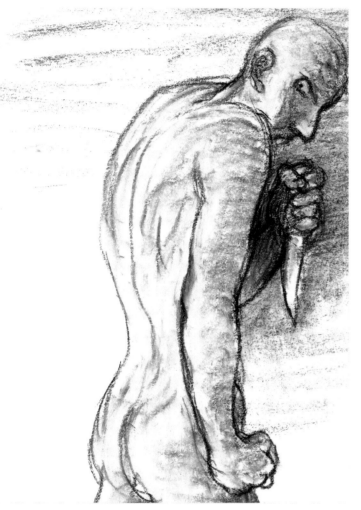

'...m sure that he would murder us all if he ...uld,' said the policeman.

'Foreigner Spreads Fear in Town,' said the newspaper in big black letters.

The people grew restless. Fear spread throughout the island.

People began to talk.
'We have to do something before it's too late!'
'We have enough troubles as it is.'
'He is not one of us. He isn't our problem.'
'He is a stranger. He doesn't belong.'
'He has to go.'

And so they went to the goat pen...

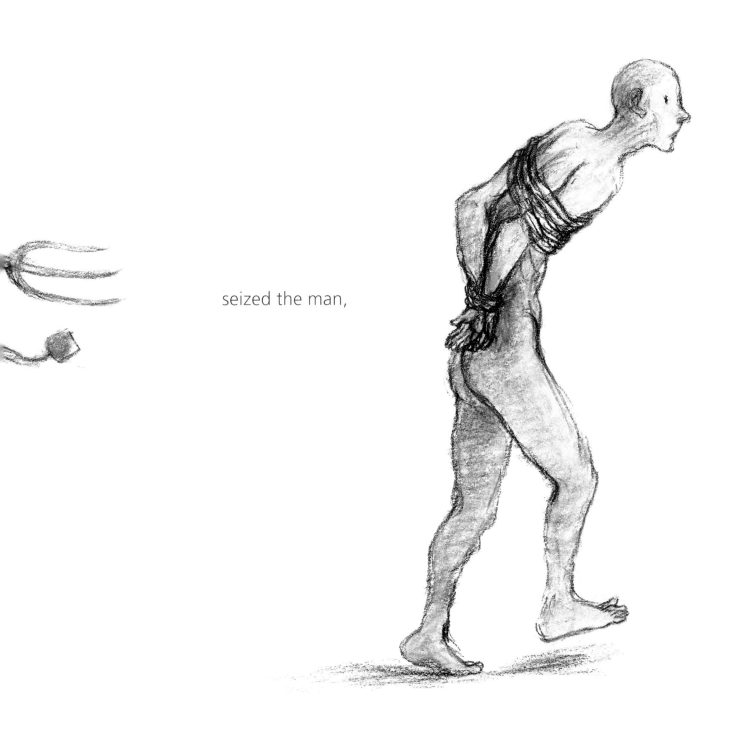

seized the man,

marched him to his raft
and pushed him out to sea.

And then they set fire to the fisherman's boat, because he had made them help the man. Some people agreed with the fisherman but the others were louder. They never again wanted to eat fish from this sea that had brought them the stranger.

And they built a great wall all around the island, with watchtowers from which they could search the sea for signs of rafts, and shoot down passing seagulls and cormorants so that no one would ever find their island again.

The Island – Awards

Prix Octogone du Livre Jeunesse, Graphic category — France, 2005

Katholischer Kinder-und Jugendbuchpreis — Germany, 2003

Die Besten Sieben, Focus, DeutschlandRadio — Germany, 2002

Eule des Monats, Bulletin Jugend & Literatur — Germany, 2002

Luchs 181, Zeit und Radio Bremen — Germany, 2002

para Victoria — A.G.

This edition published in 2007

First published in 2002 as *Die Insel* in Germany by Sauerländer Verlag.

© 2002, Patmos Verlag GmbH & Co. KG
Sauerländer Verlag, Düsseldorf

English translation copyright © Armin Greder, 2007

Allen & Unwin
83 Alexander St
Crows Nest NSW 2065
Australia
Phone: (61 2) 8425 0100
Fax: (61 2) 9906 2218
Email: info@allenandunwin.com
Web: www.allenandunwin.com

National Library of Australia
Cataloguing-in-Publication entry:

Greder, Armin.
The island.
For children.

ISBN 978 1 74175 266 3.

1. Refugees – Juvenile fiction. 2. Xenophobia – Juvenile fiction.
3. Racism – Juvenile fiction. 4.

Multiculturalism – Juvenile fiction. 5. Human rights – Juvenile fiction.
6. Picture books for children. I. Title.

833.92

Design by Armin Greder and Andrew Cunningham
Text set in 14 on 22 pt Frutiger Light
Printed in China by Everbest Printing Co Ltd

10 9 8 7 6 5 4 3

Notes for teachers are available from www.allenandunwin.com